# BUILDER GOOSE

## It's Construction Rhyme Time!

By
**BONI ASHBURN**

Illustrated by
**SERGIO DE GIORGI**

STERLING CHILDREN'S BOOKS
New York

# Here We Go 'Round the Construction Site

Here we go 'round the construction site,
construction site, construction site.
Here we go 'round the construction site
on a sunny Monday morning.

This is the way we make the plans,
tote the tools, prep the site.
This is the way we make the plans
on a sunny Monday morning.

# Hey! Diddle, Diddle

Hey! Diddle, diddle,
this hard hat is little
but needed on every job site.
If a wrench gets dropped, or a 2 by 4 falls—
you'll see why it's worn day and night.

# Simple Survey

Simple survey, measure that way,
measure this way too.
This simple survey, done today,
will show us what to do.

Measure this way for the survey—
get set up . . . we're ready!
The transit level lines things up,
the tripod holds it steady.

# One, Two, Here Comes the Crew

One, two, here comes the crew!
Three, four, here come more . . .
Five, six, pick up bricks.
Seven, eight, lay them straight.
Nine, ten, hardworking friends!

## Bump! Bump! Wheelbarrow

*Bump! Bump!* Wheelbarrow,
have you any nails?
Yes sir, yes sir,
three full pails!
One for the roofing,
one for the walls,
and one for the flooring that goes down the halls.

# Do You Know the Bulldozer?

Do you know the bulldozer,
the bulldozer, the bulldozer?
Do you know the bulldozer—
the first truck at the site?

Do you know it clears the land,
clears the land, clears the land?
The bulldozer will clear the land—
then digging can begin!

## The Itsy-Bitsy Skid Steer

The itsy-bitsy skid steer
drove up the steep dirt hill,
stockpiled rock
with nimbleness and skill.

Up came the loader
to haul it all away,
and the itsy-bitsy skid steer
kept working hard all day.

# Rat-a-tat

Rat-a-tat! Rat-a-tat! Here's the plan—
drill me a hole as fast as you can!
One more, another, until we are done,
and then we'll put anchors in every last one.

# Big Excavator

Big excavator
on the job site,
dig the hole deep
and dig the hole right!
Swing the boom here
and then over there.
Make the sides straight
and make the hole square.

# There Was an Old Foreman

There was an old foreman who ran a job site.
He had too many boulders . . . and he had dynamite!
He drilled in some holes,
put sticks in each one,
then blew up the boulders until there were none.

## Jack and Jill

Jack and Jill went up the hill
and took their lunches too.
It's time to eat
and rest their feet.
Now back to work with the crew!

# Little Jackhammer

Little jackhammer
gets all the glamour
of busting up worn-out concrete.
Gets rid of the old
(it's hard work, I'm told!),
so workers can pave the new street.

# Roll, Roll, Roll the Road

Roll, roll, roll the road,
smoothly pack it down.
'Round and around and around and around
we roll right in to town.

# It's Spinning, It's Roaring!

It's spinning, it's roaring!
It's mixing the flooring.
It tumbles around,
puts a chute to the ground,
and then it starts a-pouring.

# Crumbling Bridge Is Falling Down

Crumbling bridge is falling down,
falling down, falling down.
Crumbling bridge is falling down.
Time to fix it!

Shore it up with posts and beams!
Concrete too. Make it strong!
Crumbling bridge is falling down.
Time to fix it!

# Three Dump Trucks

Three dump trucks,
three dump trucks!
See how they work,
see how they work!
They wait in line to pick up their load
of dirt or big rocks, then they head down the road
and stop at the spot where they go to unload.
Three dump trucks.

## I'm a Heavy Grader

I'm a heavy grader, strong and stout.
Here is my blade to spread the soil out.
When I get it level, I am done.
And I'm so happy—I moved a ton!

# This Little Forklift

This little forklift carried rebar.
This little forklift hauled pipe.
This little forklift carried I-beams.
This little forklift brought bricks.
And this little forklift went
*zip, zip, zip*
all the day long.

# Heave Ho! Let's Go!

This old crane,
it swings wide!
It takes pallets for a ride.
With a *heave ho, let's go,*
swing it back for more.
Hoist it high and watch it soar!

# Crumbl-y, Rumbl-y Rock

Crumbl-y, rumbl-y rock,
the crusher crushed up the big rock.
It crushed the last one,
and then there were none.
Crumbl-y, rumbl-y rock.

# Sing a Song of Garbage

Sing a song of garbage,
a bucketful of trash.
Four and twenty loads of it—
ready to be mashed!
If you can recycle,
it's best to plan ahead.
Sort out the things you can reuse
and salvage them instead.

# Twinkle, Twinkle, Wrecking Ball

Twinkle, twinkle, wrecking ball,
in the moonlight, o'er the wall.
Back and forth you'll swing and smash,
making noises—*Wham! Bang! Crash!*
Twinkle, twinkle wrecking ball,
in the morning—look out wall!

For my dad, William Winter,
who taught me everything I know.
—B.A.

STERLING CHILDREN'S BOOKS
New York

An Imprint of Sterling Publishing
387 Park Avenue South
New York, NY 10016

STERLING CHILDREN'S BOOKS and the distinctive Sterling Children's Books logo are trademarks of Sterling Publishing Co., Inc.

ISBN 978-1-4027-7118-7

Library of Congress Cataloging-in-Publication Data

Ashburn, Boni.
 Builder Goose : it's construction rhyme time! / by Boni Ashburn ;
illustrated by Sergio De Giorgi.
  p. cm.
 Summary: Nursery rhymes are refashioned to feature construction
projects.
 ISBN 978-1-4027-7118-7
 1. Nursery rhymes. 2. Building--Juvenile poetry. 3. Construction
equipment--Juvenile poetry. 4. Children's poetry. [1. Nursery rhymes.
2. Building--Poetry. 3. Construction equipment--Poetry.] I. De Giorgi,
Sergio, ill. II. Mother Goose. III. Title.

PZ8.3.A737Bu 2011
398.8--dc22

2011004628

Distributed in Canada by Sterling Publishing
C/o Canadian Manda Group, 165 Dufferin Street, Toronto, Ontario, Canada M6K 3H6
Distributed in the United Kingdom by GMC Distribution Services, Castle Place, 166 High Street, Lewes, East Sussex, England BN7 1XU
Distributed in Australia by Capricorn Link (Australia) Pty. Ltd., P.O. Box 704, Windsor, NSW 2756, Australia

For information about custom editions, special sales, and premium and corporate purchases,
please contact Sterling Special Sales at 800-805-5489 or specialsales@sterlingpublishing.com.
Designed by Aura Fraiman Lewis

Manufactured in China
Lot #:
2 4 6 8 10 9 7 5 3 1
10/11

www.sterlingpublishing.com/kids